Old Turtle

and the Broken Truth

Old Turtle
and the Broken Truth

A Story by Douglas Wood   Watercolors by Jon J Muth

SCHOLASTIC INC.

New York Toronto London Auckland Sydney
Mexico City New Delhi Hong Kong Buenos Aires

ISBN 0-439-32110-7

12 11 10 9 8 7 6 5 4 3   5 6 7 8 9 10/0

Printed in the U.S.A.   66

First Scholastic paperback printing, January 2005

The artwork was created with watercolor and ink.
The text was set in 13-point Adobe Garamond.
Book design by David Saylor

To all who seek truths and who

listen to the language of breezes.

(And turtles.)

— Douglas Wood

Once, in a beautiful, faraway land . . .

that was, somehow, not so very far . . .

a land where every stone was a teacher

    and every breeze a language,

       where every lake was a mirror

         and every tree a ladder to the stars,

into this far and lovely land there fell . . .

a truth.

It streaked down from the stars, trailing

a tail as long as the sky.

But as it fell, it broke.

One of the pieces blazed off through the night sky,

and the other fell to earth in the beautiful land.

In the morning, Crow found the fallen piece. It seemed to be a sort of stone, shiny and pleasing to the eye. He picked it up.

"This is a lovely truth," said Crow. "I will keep it." And he carried it away. But after he had held it for awhile, and examined it closely, Crow said, "This truth does not feel quite right. A part of it is missing. I will look for a whole one." He flew off and dropped it to the ground.

Other creatures who liked shiny things soon noticed the truth as well — Fox, Coyote, Raccoon, each picked it up and carried it awhile. But they, too, found that it had rough edges and was difficult to carry, and its sparkle soon lost its appeal. "We do not need this broken truth," they said. "We will find a whole one."

Butterfly and Bear also discovered the truth, drawn by its sweetness. But each found that it left a bitter taste after all. "There is something missing in this truth," they thought. And they left it alone.

After awhile, none of the creatures even noticed the broken truth anymore, and it lay on the ground, forgotten.

Then a human being found it.

He was walking slowly, listening to breezes, gazing at beauties above and below and all around him, when he found the broken truth. On it was writing, and the writing said: "You Are Loved."

The man held it carefully, thinking it was the loveliest thing he had ever seen. He tucked the broken truth into a safe place and kept it. Sometimes he would take it out and admire it. And the truth sparkled just for him, and whispered its message to him alone. And the man thought he had never felt so proud and so happy.

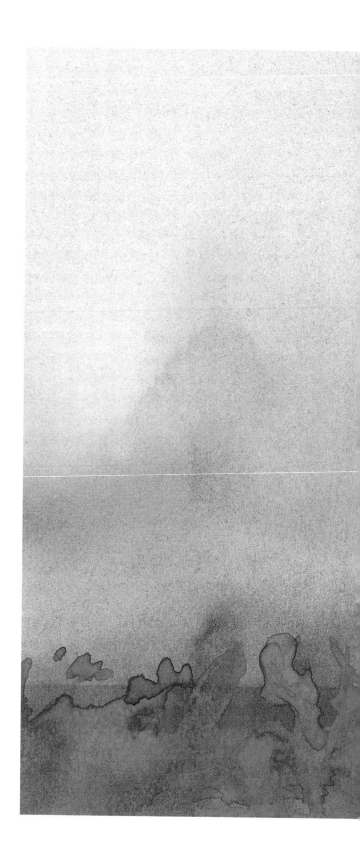

The man took the wonderful truth to his people — those who lived with him, who spoke as he spoke and dressed as he dressed and whose faces looked like his. And together they cherished their newfound truth and believed in it. They hugged it to themselves and it became their most important possession.

After awhile, the man and his people did not hear the language of breezes and stones anymore, but heard only their truth. They did not see the mirrored beauty in the lakes, or the ladders to the stars, but saw only their sparkling truth. And for them, it was enough.

And they called it . . .

The Truth.

The Truth made the people feel good and proud and strong. But soon they also began to feel fear and even anger toward those who were not like themselves and did not share their truth. The other beings and other people of the lovely land seemed less and less important. And the language of the breezes was hardly ever heard anymore.

Time passed, and *other* people said, "We must have this Great Truth for ourselves, for with it comes happiness and power."

Many battles were fought, and the broken truth was won and lost, won and lost, over and over again. But such was its power and beauty that no one ever doubted it, and when they were without it, they felt a great emptiness where their truth had been.

The stones and trees suffered. The breezes and waters suffered, and the animals, and the earth . . . . And most of all, the people suffered.

Finally, the animals went to Old Turtle —
ancient and wise as the mountains and seas
themselves. Crow and Fox went. Coyote went.
Raccoon, Butterfly, Bear, and many others. All
went to see Old Turtle.

"This truth the people quarrel over," they said,
"we have all held it ourselves. It is broken and does
not work. Please tell the people."

"I am sorry," answered Old Turtle, "but the
people will not listen. They are not yet ready."

And the suffering continued.

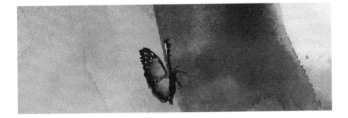

Until one day . . . a Little Girl came to find
Old Turtle. She had traveled very far, had crossed
the Mountains of Imagining and the River of
Wondering Why, had found her way through the
Forest of Finding Out. And when she had grown
tired, she had ridden on the backs of animals or the
wings of birds, and they had helped her find her
way.

Finally they came to a great hill in the very
center of the world. From there, the Little Girl
thought she had never seen so far, or seen so much
beauty.

But when she saw Old Turtle, she could hardly speak. She simply looked with eyes full of wonder.

"Why have you come so far to find me, Little One?" asked Old Turtle. Her voice rumbled like far away thunder, but was soft as the breeze through a caterpillar's whiskers.

"I . . . I wanted to ask a question," answered the Little Girl. "Where I live, the earth is sore, and people are suffering. Battles are fought, over and over again. People say it has always been this way and will never change. Can it change, Old Turtle? Can we make it change?"

Old Turtle spoke. "The world you describe is not the world that has always been, Little One."

Then Old Turtle told of how the people had found the broken truth, and the suffering it had caused.

"It is because it is so close to a great, whole truth that it has such beauty, and that the people love it so," said Old Turtle. "It is the lost portion of that broken truth that the people need, if the world is to be made whole again."

"But where is the missing piece?" asked the Little Girl. "Can we put the truth back together again?"

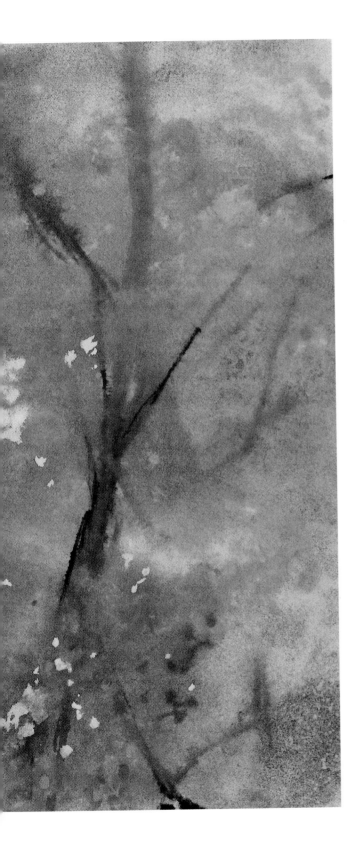

"First, my child," said Old Turtle, "remember that there are truths all around us, and within us. They twinkle in the night sky and bloom upon the earth. They fall upon us every day, silent as the snow and gentle as the rain. The people, clutching their one truth, forget that it is a part of all the small and lovely truths of life. They no longer see these truths, no longer hear them.

"But . . . perhaps, Little One, you can . . . ."

"I — I'll try," said the Little Girl.

And she thought once more of her long journey. She looked upon all the beauty that surrounded her, from the far hills to the flowers beneath her feet. She saw the movement of clouds and the soaring of birds and the dancing of light upon the green and living earth. She heard the whispering of a breeze.

And gradually . . . a feeling came over her, as though all the world were made of truths. As if the world had been made just for her and she had been made for it. And she felt a secret smile somewhere deep inside . . . and thought that, perhaps, she understood.

She looked once again at Old Turtle, her eyes more filled with wonder than before.

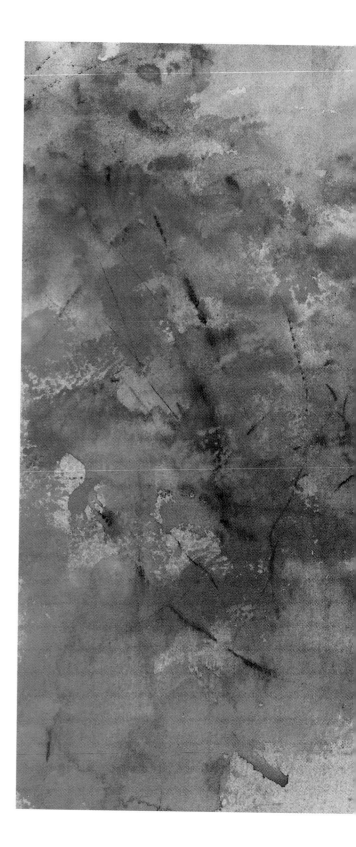

Old Turtle spoke again.

"Remember this also, Little One," she said. "The Broken Truth, and life itself, will be mended only when one person meets another — someone from a different place or with a different face or different ways — and sees and hears . . . herself. Only then will the people know that every person, every being, is important, and that the world was made for each of us."

For a long time then the two friends were quiet, high on their hill in the very center of the world. And in her heart the Little Girl thought she could see other people in other beautiful lands, people with their own ways, their own truths . . . people different from her own, but still, somehow, The People.

Finally, the Little Girl asked one more question. "Old Turtle, how will the people learn these things?"

"By seeking out those small and simple truths all around them," said Old Turtle. "By listening once more to the language of breezes, by learning lessons from stones and animals and trees and stars. Even turtles," she chuckled, "and little girls.

"Now, Little One, it is time for you to go, to return to your people and tell them what you have seen and learned, and to help them mend their Broken Truth.

"Take this with you," said Old Turtle, as she placed something in the Little Girl's hand. "I have saved it for a very long time, for someone just like you."

The Little Girl looked at what Old Turtle had given her. It was a kind of stone, a mysterious, beautiful stone. It was lovely to touch, and it made her feel good to hold it.

She squeezed it tightly, then tucked it away for her journey.

"Thank you, Old Turtle," she said, and hugged her friend's great, leathery neck.

And then she started home.

Once more she traveled through the Forest of Finding Out, crossed the River of Wondering Why and the Mountains of Imagining. Crow led the way, and again when the Little Girl grew tired, all her animal friends helped. She sometimes touched the stone Old Turtle had given her to renew her strength. And it took a long time yet almost no time at all. . . .

And she was home.

But it had been a very long journey, and those who take great journeys of the heart are changed.

The people did not recognize her. And when she spoke, they did not understand. She told them of her journey, but the people could not follow her words. She spoke of a world made of small and gentle truths, of all the peoples being one People. But they could not catch her meaning. She explained about the Broken Truth and the need to make it whole. But the people did not believe her, and could not understand.

Finally, Crow, seeing all that had happened, flew to the place high above the village where the Great Truth was kept, in a place where all could see it. He cawed and cawed in his loudest voice. And suddenly the Little Girl knew what to do. She climbed to the high place herself. She took Old Turtle's stone from her pocket and . . . carefully . . . added the missing piece to the old, broken one.

The fit was perfect.

The people looked.

And looked.

And looked.

Some frowned.

Some smiled.

Some even laughed.

And some cried.

And they began to understand.

Time passed and upon the beautiful land the trees climbed like ladders to the stars, the waters shone like mirrors, and the people saw their beauty. A breeze stirred and they heard its music. Tiny truths fell by day and night, gentle as the rain and snow, and the people found them and kept them in their hearts.

And slowly, as the people met other people different from themselves, they began to see . . . themselves.

And far away, on a hill

in the very center of the world . . .

Old Turtle smiled.